Man's Best Friend

Other books by James Mitchum Oates:

Life 101 – A True Life Story

The Revolution

With Cream Cheese Please

A Classic Tale from the Streets

The Silent Deception

Tale of Henry Tinsdale

Man's Best Friend

James Mitchum Oates

Copyright © 2020 by James Mitchum Oates.

ISBN:	Softcover	978-1-9845-8652-0
	eBook	978-1-9845-8651-3

All rights reserved. No part of this book may be reproduced or transmitted in any form or by any means, electronic or mechanical, including photocopying, recording, or by any information storage and retrieval system, without permission in writing from the copyright owner.

This is a work of fiction. Names, characters, places and incidents either are the product of the author's imagination or are used fictitiously, and any resemblance to any actual persons, living or dead, events, or locales is entirely coincidental.

Any people depicted in stock imagery provided by Getty Images are models, and such images are being used for illustrative purposes only.
Certain stock imagery © Getty Images.

Print information available on the last page.

Rev. date: 06/29/2020

To order additional copies of this book, contact:
Xlibris
1-888-795-4274
www.Xlibris.com
Orders@Xlibris.com

To you, Lacy. You are a true friend indeed. You are sorely missed.

FOREWORD

People come and go on a daily basis not knowing when their time will come – to expire back to the dust in which they came. Also people take for granted the life that we have in the here and now. Instead of trying to cherish every day, every moment that we do have here, because life is promised to no one, we squander and waste life. The "could've", "should've", and "would've" should stop being a part of our mental routine and replaced with, "I did".

The average life span of a dog is seven years in the aging process to every one year of a human. That gives these creatures a lot less time for life in comparison to humans. And in that time, dogs can serve humans very well. If trained properly, they can be a service to the disabled, they can be watchers or protectors of your resident, they can serve in a law enforcement unit, or they can just be good friends and companions. However dogs are utilized is in the sole power of its master. Just the same with our own lives; however we choose to live or become what we want is up to us. So in relation to the things within our control, there's no pointing the finger and blaming anyone for you misfortunes. It's all on you. Then you have the dog who is what he is because of his master. This is man's loyal companion – man's true best friend.

ONE

Jake and Elizabeth Rigsby have the most loving relationship ever. They have the most compassionate love for one another that if one were to analyze their relationship, that person might say that their bond is unusual – unusually strong. For example, when they have an argument or disagreement, they don't stay angry at each other very long because they come right back to each other with apologies and hugs and kisses.

They both have so much in common and think along the same lines. One notion they both strongly agree upon is the idea of love at first sight. They both feel that this is a very real concept because it happened to the both of them for each other. Jake was in his mid-twenties when one day he was coming out of the grocery store, looking down and not paying attention, when someone bumped into him almost knocking the groceries out of his hands. Immediately Jake got angry and started to exclaim, "Why don't you watch where you're going?" even though it was his fault.

But before he could get all of the words out, he stopped in mid-sentence and was just entranced. He stood there staring at the person who bumped into him. And then she found herself staring at him as well.

First she apologized and then he apologized and then that led to conversation. This conversation led to an exchange of phone numbers which then led to dating. This dating led to intimacy which finally led to the two of them on the alter getting married. But they both say it was the same feeling for both of them – love at first sight. One way Jake knew it was love at first sight was because when she bumped into him and he saw her, the feeling he had was undescribable. It was way more than a physical lust.

Elizabeth felt the same way.

As a matter of fact, it was less a physical lust than anything. It was just a burning deep in both of their hearts.

And after so long a time from when they first met, they finally told each other how they felt about one another and from there, their love began to grow. But in that magic moment when they did first meet, once they decided to get married, they both agreed to get married on the same time and date in which they first met – May 19th at 4:50 p.m. This was done so that every year when their marriage anniversary comes up, they can feel that same special feeling as to when they met.

This is their third anniversary. They're both in the living room.

"Come on, babe. You know I get anxious when you make me wait like this," I said with my eyes closed sitting on the couch.

"Just a second, honey. I have to go outside and get it," Elizabeth responded.

"Alright I'll wait."

Suddenly Elizabeth left out the front door and then came back in in ten seconds.

"Alright you can open your eyes," she joyfully exclaimed.

When I did open my eyes, I saw her standing there holding the cutest puppy in her arms rubbing its fur.

"Oh honey, you didn't…" I said in amazement. This is great! When'd you get him?"

"It's a her. And I picked her out last week."

"Let me hold her," I said reaching out for the puppy.

There I held it in my arms, stroking its fur.

"What are we going to name her?"

"I was thinking about Penny."

"Sounds good to me."

TWO

"Alright honey, I guess I'll see you this afternoon," Elizabeth said standing at the door with her jacket on and purse in hand.

She was on her way to work.

"Alright babe."

"Now listen, you have the money, right?"

"Yep, right here," I said patting my left pants pocket.

"Alright honey," she said leaning in for a kiss.

Their kisses were always so magical.

Then she was out the door.

As soon as I closed the door behind her, my stomach started grumbling.

Breakfast time.

I went into the kitchen and the first thing that caught my eye was on top of the refrigerator – Frosted Flakes. Then I thought, "Naw," as I walked to the cabinet past the refrigerator and opened it up. I looked and saw a box of Hamburger Helper.

"This'll be good for tonight," I said to myself taking the box down from the top shelf.

Then I looked more until I came across oatmeal.

Oh hell no!

Then I remembered, Elizabeth bought that because she wanted me to try different foods, even the ones I don't like.

Then I found a box of pancakes.

No, probably not.

I just wanted something simple.

So I went back to the refrigerator and opened it up.

"Ah, here we go," I thought to myself as I saw the carton of eggs. I took them out and went and got a bowl. As I whipped them up, I thought to myself, "not too much salt." Then when they were done, I got a plate and put them on it and set it on the table.

The bread was on the table so I opened it and took out two pieces and carried them to the toaster. While they were cooking, I went to the refrigerator and got the orange juice out and got a cup.

My intent was to only pour half a cup, but when I started pouring, I just kept pouring until it was full.

Then my toast was done.

Next, I went back to the refrigerator and found the strawberry jam. I got my toast and utensils and was ready to feast. I put my toast on the plate, set my utensils down, pulled my chair back and sat down and didn't waste any time.

When I was done, I took my dishes to the sink. I didn't bother to wash them.

They'll get done – later.

Then I dug my hand in my left pants pocket to make sure the money was there. I pulled out five $20 bills.

"Yep, it's all there," I said to myself, then shoved it back in.

As I walked out of the kitchen, I noticed I felt tired. Then before I knew it, I was yawning.

Maybe I didn't get enough sleep last night. I stayed up past twelve playing with Penny.

So I headed to the bedroom.

When I got there, nothing ever looked more appealing than my unmade bed. I took my shoes off, climbed in and got under the covers. About five seconds after my eyes were closed, I remembered, "I have to set the alarm clock so I can wake up and get to the store."

I set it to wake me up at 11:30 a.m. Then I pulled the covers over my head.

Suddenly I was nine-years-old again. I was running down the street hard and fast. I was running so fast, I felt like my heart was going to burst out any second. Why was I running so fast? I wasn't running like that for no reason. I was being chased. Frank Manfred and his friends were chasing me one day after school. You see, today was a usual typical day at school until about 11:50 a.m. when Frank accused me of liking boys. This is when I called his mother a cock-sucker. And so it lead to this. I felt like my life was on the line. So I ran. I ran like I never did and probably never would again if I survived.

But then they caught me.

I ran down a street with a dead-end cut-off.

They surrounded me.

As they got closer and closer, the only thing I could do was pray. Then I felt a fist slam into my right jaw. Next a punch to the stomach. And then I was down. I covered my head as the kicks and punches came more and more.

Then through all of their screaming at me, I heard yelling. But the yelling came from a different person. Soon the punches and kicks became less as the yelling grew more.

I finally recognized that the yelling was my brother's voice. I looked up to see him fighting off my attackers.

As the boys surrounded him, without looking at me, he yelled, "Get the hell outta here, Jake!"

Without thought, I hopped up and ran past the boys. I ran and ran until I finally stopped to turn and look back. I stood there for a second. He was holding his own very well for a while. But then the numbers caught up to him. They proved too much for him. Soon he was on the ground and they were on him.

"No," I whispered to myself.

Then, almost as if being controlled, I turned and ran.

I ran home.

Luckily dad was home and I told him what happened. We hopped in the truck and drove to where Caleb was at. When we got there, the boys were gone. But there was Caleb – in a bloody mess on the ground.

We hopped out of the truck and ran to him. He looked at us and tried to speak, but couldn't. I burst out into tears as I hovered over his body.

"Caleb, I'm sorry. This is all my fault."

"There's no time for that now. Help me get him in the truck."

We carried him and put him in the truck and dad drove to the nearest hospital.

When we got him in, they took Caleb back and dad and I had to wait in the waiting room.

We waited in silence.

Sometime later, the doctor came out and said we could see him. When we got to his room, we saw he was bandaged up almost all over.

The doctor then said, "He's got some broken ribs, a broken wrist, a cracked femur, and a few concussions. Can someone tell me how this happened?"

Then I spoke up, "It's my fault. He was protecting me. There were some boys trying to beat me up and Caleb came to my rescue."

"Why were these boys trying to beat you up?"

"I called one of their moms a cock-sucker."

The doctor then replied, "So your brother went through all of this because you called someone's mother a cock-sucker?"

I didn't know what to say. I looked over at dad who had the strangest look on his face. Even though I couldn't quite understand what his expression meant, one expression I could definitely pick up on was disappointment.

He just sat there with that look on his face looking at me. He started to say something.

Then the alarm went off.

The dream happened exactly as I remembered it so it seemed as if I were there again.

I turned the alarm off and then hopped up and put my shoes on. Then Penny came up to me, tail wagging and licking my hand. I played with her for a little bit and then glanced over at the clock.

It said 11:38 a.m.

"I better get going," I said to myself.

I then stood up, headed to the closet and grabbed a light jacket, grabbed my car keys off of the drawer, and headed for the door.

As I tried to get out of the door, Penny tried to follow. I kept pushing her back in with my foot until I was able to get the door closed.

Then I headed to the car.

When I got in, I checked my pockets to make sure I still had the money. Then I thought, "Am I missing anything?" I felt in my other pocket and fumbled with the house keys and then pulled out the list Elizabeth gave me. I put it back in my pocket, started the car up, and then was headed for Wal-mart.

Traffic was pretty light so in no time at all, I was there. I found a parking space and went in.

As soon as I got in, I grabbed a cart, then pulled the list out.

The first thing on the list was bananas, and I was right in the fruit section. I searched through the bananas until I found a good bunch – not too ripe.

I put it in the cart and looked on the list for the next item.

It said orange juice.

The orange juice was on the other side of the store. As I began to make the journey, I came across the pet aisle. My curiosity heightened as to what I could find for Penny. I began walking down that aisle and saw all kinds of things from chew toys, to leashes, to dog treats.

I figured if I could just get a few of these things for Penny, it could really save on having to get it later. So I started putting things in my cart – whatever looked good for puppies. In no time at all, my cart was just about loaded with puppy supplies.

I looked in my cart and then thought to myself, "I'd better at least get the orange juice. So after I got that, I got in the check-out line.

When the cashier was done ringing everything up, my total came to $98.34.

I had just enough.

Being very pleased with myself, I took the cart out to the car and loaded up the trunk with the stuff.

Then I got in and drove home.

When I got home, I brought everything in the house. The first thing I did was put up the bananas and orange juice. Then Penny came running up to me and I bent down and began rubbing her ears.

"Look what I got for you," I said pulling out a bag of puppy treats. I opened them and then fed them to her one by one.

Then I played with her for a while and lost track of time.

Before long I heard a key in the door. In came Elizabeth.

"Hey honey."

"Hey babe. How was your day at work?" I asked.

"Oh stressful as usual."

"Babe, come over here. I want to show you what I bought for Penny."

She came over and began looking through the bags.

"Where are all the groceries you were supposed to get?" she said rummaging through the bags.

"Well I saw all of these wonderful things for puppies so I got them for Penny."

"But what about the food for the house?" she said with obvious irritation in her voice. "Did you even get the chicken and rice? I was going to make a surprise dinner for tonight of the chicken and rice casserole."

"No, I didn't. Which is why I was thinking you could give me more money tomorrow and I could go back and get the food."

She stood there looking at me with a blank expression. But one thing I could definitely detect in those eyes was anger and disappointment.

THREE

That night, instead of the chicken and rice casserole, we had hamburger helper. And then we went to bed. Also I think she wanted to be intimate that night. Just a nice quiet evening with a nice dinner and the two of us alone.

I'm sorry, babe.

Soon afterward, I began to regret that event more than I thought I would. For days it seemed like we were growing more distant and apart. Then days became weeks.

I bought her a box of chocolates and a set of flowers to show how much I cared. And for the most part, she seemed to like them.

But something was missing. That magic we had when we were around each other was dwindling.

I was confused.

"Babe, we need to talk," I announced one afternoon.

"About what?" she responded.

"About us. Where are we going? Why are we growing so distant?"

"What are you talking about?"

"It seems as if ever since that incident with the groceries that day, we've been falling out."

"Jake honey, we're not falling out. It's just that I've been more tired lately."

This seemed reasonable so I said, "Oh, well I was thinking how about we go see that new Jason Statham movie tonight?"

"Oh not tonight, honey. Didn't I tell you I have to be up early tomorrow to meet with a client about his funds?"

"No, you didn't."

"Yeah, apparently his money is somehow being transferred to the wrong bank. Imagine that."

"Yeah, imagine that."

After dinner, I fed Penny and walked her. Elizabeth had already gone to sleep. When I got outside, the crisp air hitting my skin felt so good that I just wanted to stay out there for a while. But I had other things to do.

When I came in, I put Penny in her cage. Then I went into the bedroom and put my night clothes on, careful not to wake Elizabeth. Feeling tired, I began to yawn. But I wasn't going to bed, not yet. I had some things I had to sort out.

I went into the living room and sat on the couch. I began to think of when we first met and that spark of love when we first saw each other. It was this same spark that sustained us through the years. Then I thought about how distant we had grown recently. What else could I think other than that she was having an affair? I had no reason to think this. But nothing's the same as it used to be. The excitement is gone. Even the passion in our lovemaking had become less. Could it be that there is someone who is making love to her better than I do? Or perhaps someone who makes her feel alive again?

I just don't know.

Well I'll find out tomorrow. She's not expecting me to follow her to work. If I catch her in the act, I'll just confront the two of them.

But then what?

I don't want to leave her because I still do love her dearly even if she doesn't feel the same for me anymore.

I'll just confront them and put on a big show as if I'm very angry and irate. Hopefully I can scare the guy off and we can work on getting our life back on track.

I then noticed I was nodding off. So I decided to go on to bed. When I got to the bedroom, I saw Elizabeth lying there peacefully. I wanted to kiss her on the cheek, but somehow I knew she wouldn't even feel it. So I climbed in bed and went to sleep.

I awakened in the morning to hear water running. Elizabeth was taking her shower getting ready for work.

Then I became nervous. Nervous because today I would confront her other lover if there was one. I didn't want to eat or anything else. All I could do was get dressed and get ready. I went into the living room and sat on the couch and tried to look inconspicuous – as if I weren't up to anything. About thirty minutes later, she came into the living room. She was dressed and ready to go.

"Alright honey, I'll see you soon," she announced as she approached the door.

"Alright babe."

Then she was out. Neither one of us noticed that we both forgot the kiss goodbye.

As soon as I heard the car start, I grabbed my car keys and headed out.

As I followed her, I said to myself, "This is not the route she normally takes to her job. Finally she parked into the parking lot of a hospital. She got out of the car and went in.

I sat across the street and watched. After about forty minutes, I decided to go in. Just as I got to the door, she came out.

"Oh, there you are," I retorted. "So this is where your new lover is – a hospital?"

She looked at me with the saddest eyes and replied, "I have stage four lung cancer and an expected time of seven weeks to live."

She then got in her car and drove off.

FOUR

There I stood – breathless for a moment.

What did she just say?

My first inclination upon hearing that was to go right in that hospital and find that son-of- a bitch that's been sleeping with my wife and punch him right in the face. I had totally disregarded what she just told me because I would never, in a million years, want to believe that what she said was true.

Snap out of it and go get your wife!

I immediately ran to my car and hopped in. I pulled the keys out and as I tried to start it up, I fumbled and just couldn't do it.

"Goddamit!" I yelled as I slammed my hands against the steering wheel. Then the tears began to roll down my face as the notion that what she said was more than likely real.

There was no other lover.

There was something much worse than that in our lives now. And it threatened to take my Elizabeth away from me in about seven weeks.

I sat there and cried and cried for about another minute just dreading this reality.

Then I said out loud, "I have to go to her and comfort her and hold her and just be with her."

Then I started the car up and headed home. I didn't know if that was where she was going, but I figured I'd just go there.

When I got home, Penny came running up to me.

"Not now," I mumbled. And as if she got the message, she went elsewhere. I felt as if I hadn't been to sleep in ten years. But instead of going to sleep, I sat on the couch and waited – for my wife. I wanted her to walk through that door and I could go to her and look her in the eyes and tell her that everything would be just fine and then seven weeks later she would be the same happy and healthy Elizabeth that I fell in love with and that damn doctor was wrong.

Hours passed and still no Elizabeth. Finally I heard the key in the door. In came Elizabeth; but she had a grin on her face.

"Elizabeth, are you O.K.?" I asked in a baffled tone.

"Jake honey, I'm fine."

"Are you sure? Back at the hospital earlier today…" I said still confused.

"Jake darling, don't you see? I'm already dead."

Then she lunged for me.

I hopped up from my sleep and screamed, "No!" Then there was the sound of a key in the door. And in came Elizabeth. She ran to me and hugged me. Then Penny came in and jumped up on the couch and started licking Elizabeth's face. Just the three of us being there, comforting each other, let me know it was not a dream.

"We'll get through this," I said caressing her hair. "I'm sorry for what I said and thought that you were having an affair. I should've known better."

"Babe, I would never cheat on you. You're the only one for me. But now we have to deal with this head on."

"Yeah babe, about that. I was thinking how about we don't deal with it."

"What?" she said looking at me perplexed.

"Let's just leave it in the hands of the Lord. But we have to have faith. I was reading something somewhere a couple of months ago where there was a man diagnosed with brain cancer and he had an expected time of eleven weeks left to live. What he did was he refused all medical treatment and instead went to a healing ministry. He told them the diagnosis and how long he had to live. The minister then blessed him and healed him through God's power. No one believed the man was healed. But then twenty-five years later, he came back to the same doctor that told him he had eleven weeks to live and said, "Now what do you have to say?"

"Jake, you can't believe everything you read. We have to be practical."

"Practical? I'm being as practical as I can. You know that if you go through chemo-therapy, it won't do anything for you."

"It may give me more time. And right now, that's the best we can hope for."

"I just don't want to lose you," I said hugging her tightly and rubbing her back.

Suddenly something seemed strange. Then I looked to my right and then left and then all around me. Penny was gone and the front door was open. Elizabeth left it open when she came in.

"Penny…, here Penny," I said standing up headed to the front door. I feared the worst.

Then there she came in through the door, wagging her tail. I picked her up and began kissing and rubbing her.

"There you are. You scared me for a moment. I thought you were going to leave me forever. I don't ever want you to go."

Elizabeth stood there looking at me. The tears had welled up in her eyes. She thought I had gone crazy.

FIVE

That next morning while Elizabeth slept, I decided to call Caleb.

"Hello."

"Hey Caleb. It's Jake."

"Oh hey, Jake. What's up?"

"Well not much. Just that my wife has stage four lung cancer and about seven weeks to live."

I heard Caleb snort a laugh and then replied, "Come on, Jake. That's not so funny."

Then he could hear me crying on the other end.

"Oh my God, you're serious."

"What did I do to deserve this?" I said bawling into the phone.

"Jake, I'm on my way."

"No, no please. Shelly and the kids need you there. Just do me a favor and pray for us."

"I'll be praying everyday and every night. You sure you don't want me to come? I'm only three hours away."

"No, just kiss Shelly and the kids for me."

"Alright Jake."

"And Caleb, I'm sorry – for everything."

I didn't have to go into detail what I was sorry about. Caleb knew exactly what I meant.

"It's O.K., Jake."

"Alright, love you."

"Love you too, little bro."

"Bye."

"Bye."

After I hung up, I put my head in my hands.

"Why is this happening? How?" I thought.

I really didn't know how. She was not a smoker. So how did she end up with lung cancer? I decided to ask her.

I got up and went to the bedroom. When I got there, she was sitting on the bed just staring at the floor. I went to her and sat beside her and put my arm around her and then gave her a kiss on the cheek.

Without looking at me or responding to the kiss, she said, "You know when I was a little girl my role models were my grandparents. They were so in love with each other. Because they loved each other so much, they stayed together a long time. I don't remember how old she was when my grandmother finally passed away. But both she and he were very old and had lived full lives of love and happiness."

"What happened to your grandfather?"

"He died sometime shortly after she did of a broken heart. But all of the time they spent together and all of the love they had made me want to be like them and have a love like theirs someday."

Finally looking at me, she said, "Jake honey, I love you. I really do. But the truth is we don't have much time left together. All we have is what we have now – each other."

"I'm just so confused. Did the doctor tell you how you got lung cancer? You don't smoke."

He told me that there are different ways you can get lung cancer. And he's not exactly sure how I got it either. But he told me that if they could have detected it earlier in its first stages, they could've done a lot more."

Then she hugged me and looked me directly in the eyes and said, "If I could leave a piece of me here with you, I would."

Then Penny came trotting in the room and came up to my feet and started licking my toes. I then picked her up and began caressing her and talking to her.

"I think I already have done that exactly," Elizabeth thought.

SIX

"I'll tell you one thing," I said after Penny left the room, "I say we should go talk to this doctor who said you have lung cancer. I mean it could be a wrong diagnosis."

"His name is Dr. Marshfield and he's pretty certain that he's not mistaken. He showed me the X-rays where the cancer has deteriorated my lungs. Also I decided that the last time I was there would in fact be the last time I went there for fear of any more bad news."

"How much worse could it be than this?"

"Right."

"How about we stop focusing on how bad it is and try to enjoy the time we do have left together?"

"I agree."

"So let's say we have a nice breakfast and then go and do something. It's a wonderful day."

"Yeah, that sounds great. How about we go to the park and then to the movies?"

"O.K., now we're talking."

"I'll tell you what, I'll hop in the shower and while I'm doing that, you can be making breakfast."

"O.K. sure."

She then leaned in for a kiss. Something about that kiss reminded me of the magic that was there in our old kisses.

I then stood up and headed for the kitchen. Five minutes later, I heard the shower water running.

I stood there looking at the stove for a minute thinking to myself, "Now what should I cook?" all the while knowing that whatever I cooked had to be good.

Then I made my way to the cabinet. When I opened it, I saw all kinds of things. Then I saw a bag of rice.

"That's a good start," I thought to myself.

So I pulled that down. Then I saw a box of grits.

"That'll do also. Now let's see what we can find in the fridge." I went over and opened it up and the first thing I saw was the eggs.

Excellent!

I pulled those out and said, "Now just one more thing. Ah, here we go," I exclaimed as I pulled out the bacon.

Then I went and pulled out the skillets and pots so I could cook everything at one time.

While I was cooking, the aroma filled the entire house. I finally heard the water stop running in the bathroom as Elizabeth replied, "Smells good, honey."

Soon enough she came in the kitchen fully dressed. And waiting for her there on the table was a plate of rice, grits, bacon, eggs, and a cup of orange juice to wash it all down with.

And there was mine next to hers.

She sat down and I sat down too.

Normally Elizabeth and I weren't church-going folks, neither did we usually say grace before meals. But as if it were automatic and a part of our daily routine, we both bowed our heads and closed our eyes before eating.

Then I began:

"Dear Heavenly Father,

We thank You for everything You have blessed us with. From our families, to Penny, to each other, and to this wonderful meal. Lord, today we ask that You strengthen us in our troubled time. Give us the guidance to know what we have to do and the serenity to do it. We thank You for the love we have to cherish for one another, the time we have spent together, and the time we have left together."

Then I heard her say, "Amen," as she thought the prayer was done. With my head still bowed and my eyes still closed, I took hold of her hand.

"And also, Lord," I began again, "I would just like to add that may You help us find each other in the next life so that we can fall in love and spend precious time together just like in this life. These things we pray for. Amen."

I then opened my eyes and saw her looking at me.

"That was beautiful," she responded.

"Thanks babe. Now let's dig in."

We ate in silence, but one thing was for sure, we both enjoyed our meal.

Once we were done, I took the dishes and put them in the sink.

"I'll do the dishes while you get ready."

"O.K. I'll just hop in the shower real quick. I won't be long."

I went to the bedroom and got some clothes laid out. Then I went to the bathroom.

I had a nice long shower. When I was done, I went to the bedroom to get dressed.

"Honey, are you ready?" I called out from the bedroom.

I waited for a response for about ten seconds. When I didn't hear anything, I figured she didn't hear me.

So I called out, "Honey…"

No response.

I went to the kitchen to see her lying on the floor by the sink.

"Oh my God!" I exclaimed as I rushed to her.

I took my phone out and dialed 9-1-1.

Was I too late?

I already knew the answer to that question.

I just wish I was better prepared for it.

SEVEN

I felt for a pulse.

Nothing.

"No, no, stay with me," I cried out as I held her head up. A few minutes later, I heard the sirens.

I let them in and showed them where she was at. When they came to her, one of them put his finger on her wrist to check her pulse.

"How long has she been unconscious?" he asked.

"I don't know. For a while," I responded.

Then he tried CPR for a while.

She was still unresponsive.

"Please tell me she's not dead."

"I'm sorry."

It was a nice funeral. Both Caleb and Shelly were there. Every now and then I would steal a glance at Caleb. But then the last glance I stole I saw him just staring at me. Most of the time while the funeral was in session, I was drifted off. I was focused on the exact moment when after I followed Elizabeth that day and she came out of the hospital and told me she had lung cancer with seven weeks to live.

The way I felt upon hearing that.

And I thought she had another lover. How could I have been so naïve?

Finally the funeral was over. We said our good-byes and that was that.

Then me, Caleb, and Shelly drove to my house.

When we got there, I sat on the couch and began crying again. Shelly came and sat next to me and began comforting me.

"It's O.K. We're here for you," she soothingly said while rubbing my back.

Then Penny came up to Caleb and began licking his shoe.

"Hey, who's this?" he said while bending down to pick her up.

"That's Penny. Elizabeth bought her on our anniversary. She's all I have left."

Caleb then put Penny down and came and sat next to me on the couch.

"You're going to beat this," he said. "You just have to know she's in a better place."

"You know we were trying to have children. Caleb, if you could do me a favor. But it's going to sound a little weird."

"Sure, whatever you need."

"If you and Shelly could just give me time to myself to work things out on my own. Now is the time for me to get up and get on with my life. I need to find a job and just get myself together."

"Oh, you want us to go home?"

"Please."

"Alright, but first we want to make sure you're O.K. and that you have everything you need."

"Oh, I don't really need anything. Just you and Shelly coming was good for me."

"Alright bro," Caleb said standing up.

Then Shelly stood up. "If you need anything, I mean anything, don't hesitate to call."

"Thanks guys. I love you."

"Love you too, bro," Caleb said standing by the door.

"Take care of yourself," Shelly said walking to the door.

With that, they were gone.

EIGHT

Days passed. And as they did, I think I fed Penny more than myself.

All I did was sleep – sleep the pain away.

Till one morning I decided to give Dr. Marshfield a visit. This all happened so fast and I wanted some answers. So I got up, had a shower, got dressed, and was out the door.

I didn't eat breakfast.

I got in the car and headed to the hospital where Elizabeth gave me the news that changed my life forever.

When I got there, I got out and went in. I went to the receptionist and told her I needed to see Dr. Marshfield. She asked my reason for wanting to see him and I told her about the situation with Elizabeth and that I was her husband.

She then replied, "Just a second," and got on the phone.

"Yes, Dr. Marshfield, there's a Jake Rigsby here to see you. He says he was Elizabeth Rigsby's husband."

Then a pause.

"O.K. I'll send him up now. Dr. Marshfield will see you now," she said hanging up the phone. "He's in room 302."

"Thank you," I said headed to the elevator.

I was on my way to see the man who said my wife had lung cancer and seven weeks to live. In a way I was already angry at him before even meeting him. Angry because he certainly could've done more to save my wife's life.

But that's ridiculous because I already know he did all he could probably.

Although one thing's for certain, he did say she had an estimated time of seven weeks to live and that certainly wasn't seven weeks.

But did it really matter? She was going to die anyway.

Then I reached the third floor. I got off the elevator and headed to room 302.

When I got there I didn't knock. I just walked in.

I saw a tall, brown-haired man sitting in a chair staring out the window.

"Dr. Marshfield?" I said.

"Yes, you must be Jake Rigsby. Please sit down," he said motioning me to the chair across from him.

"Alright, I'll get right to it because I have some questions that need to be answered. First of all how did she even get lung cancer? She was not a smoker."

"That's a good question. Unfortunately I don't have an answer. You see, there are several ways you can get it. It can come from any number of different factors."

"Well what about the fact that you said she had seven weeks to live? That wasn't seven weeks."

"Seven weeks was just an estimated time. It was seven weeks tops. I was giving her the benefit of the doubt."

"I see."

"Mr. Rigsby, I know this is hard for you, but…"

"No, please don't do that. You have no idea how hard this is for me."

"Believe me, I do," he said with a more subtle tone. "I lost my father to brain cancer two years ago."

"Oh no."

"Yes," he said placing his hand on my shoulder. "Losing someone is always hard. But it's how we deal with it once they're gone that counts."

I looked directly in his eyes. I thought I saw his eyes begin to water a little.

"Just one more thing," I said. "Did she mention me much?"

"Oh, very often. She described you as the love of her life."

And here I thought she was having an affair. How could I?

"That's nice to know."

"But remember, it's what you do once they're gone that counts."

"You're exactly right," I said standing up and heading for the door.

"Where are you going?"

"To find a job."

NINE

The first place I decided to try was United Global Finance Company. The main word in that title was "Finance." I figured my Associate's Degree in finance would definitely come in handy. I pulled into the parking lot of the big building, parked the car, got out and went in.

The first thing I noticed when I went in was the temperature. It was much cooler inside than outside. Next I noticed the number of people all dressed up just passing by and not noticing anything else – certainly not me.

I walked up to the receptionist desk.

"Hi, I'd like an application please," I said to the lady behind the desk.

She looked me up and down as if pre-judging me as to what kind of applicant I would make. Then she reached into a drawer to her right and pulled out some papers. She looked at each one and replied, "Just fill these out," as she handed them to me.

"Thank you," I said taking the forms. Then I turned and left.

When I got home and walked through the door, I felt like something was missing.

It was Elizabeth; the only thing I had in my life. Then Penny came up to me wagging her tail. This was the only thing I had in my life now.

"There you are," I said bending down to pet her. Then I stopped myself because I didn't want to get so wrapped up playing with Penny and neglect what was important – filling out my application. I went to the kitchen. There was an ink pen on the table. So I sat down and began.

When I got to the section about the experience I had, I thought it best to exaggerate the truth a bit.

Finally I was done. I decided to drop it off first thing tomorrow morning. Starting to feel tired, I began to yawn. I went to the bedroom, took my shoes off, climbed in bed, and pulled the covers over my head.

Soon enough I was coming out of a store and not paying attention to where I was going. I bumped into someone – Elizabeth. It was happening exactly as it had the day I met her. My dreams were becoming more precise and concrete lately. The only thing is with this dream, it was as if it were being shown to me. I was there, but it was like I was a spectator watching everything happen again. It was like I was above both me and Elizabeth looking down on us seeing how it happened.

The next thing I knew, I was watching Elizabeth taking off her bra while I sat there on the bed looking at her.

This was the first time we made love.

She then took off the rest of her garments and I was already naked. She then turned the lights out and came and got in the bed. As we indulged in each other, I remember me so badly wanting to say, "I love you."

But was it too early? This was our first time making love.

Until finally it just came out. "I love you," I moaned.

"What?" she said.

"I love you," I said again knowing it was too late to take it back.

"Do you love me?" I asked.

"It's too soon to tell," she responded.

The next thing I knew, we were on the altar getting married. I never looked so handsome in a suit in all my life. And Elizabeth was absolutely gorgeous – a radiant beauty.

Then we kissed.

There was something in that kiss that said, "I'm yours forever."

But then I was in the kitchen with Elizabeth the day I was supposed to go grocery shopping and instead I bought all of that stuff for Penny. I saw the disappointment and frustration on her face. And then I remembered how everything just got bad from that point. Is that the reason Elizabeth got lung cancer and left me alone?

No, that's ridiculous.

Next I was sitting down with Elizabeth talking to her sometime after I had found out she had cancer. She then said, "If I could leave a piece of me here with you, I would."

It was then and there I realized she had in fact left a piece of her with me – through Penny.

TEN

When I awakened, the first thing I realized is how hungry I was. I got up and went to the kitchen to see what I could find. When I got there, I noticed the Frosted Flakes on top of the refrigerator. Even though it was past breakfast time, that would suffice just fine. But then I remembered what Elizabeth had told me about eating foods sometimes that I didn't care for. So I made my way to the cabinet.

When I opened it, the first thing that caught my eye was the oatmeal. I absolutely hated oatmeal.

Perfect!

I took it out, got a pot and cooked a nice big bowl of it. Then I got a cup of orange juice and was ready to enjoy my meal.

As I ate, I did so with great confidence that Elizabeth was smiling down on me from heaven.

She would be proud that I took her advice.

When I was done, I took my dishes to the sink and washed them. Suddenly I heard Penny barking and whimpering in the living room. I went to go see what was going on. When I got there, I saw her just standing stoutly fully attentive at the front door, just whining.

Then I figured it out.

She was waiting on Elizabeth to come through that door.

"I miss her too," I said picking Penny up and then walking to the couch.

I sat down holding Penny and before I could start crying, I told myself, "No, no more tears. It's time to move on."

I put Penny down and went and got her food and water and set them out. When she was done, I got her leash and we went for a walk.

The air outside was crisp and nice and let me know that yes, there was in fact reason to live on and be at peace. I wished I could have stayed out there all day long.

But I couldn't.

I had to go grocery shopping.

When I got to the house, I put Penny in her cage, grabbed my wallet and car keys and headed back out the door. I got to the car and then headed to the store. When I got there, I had no trouble finding a parking space. So I parked and went in.

When I walked in, I grabbed a cart and the first thing I saw was Oreo Cookies on sale.

And I loved Oreos.

So I put them in my cart.

From there it was easy sailing because a lot of the things I liked were on sale. Soon my cart was half-way full of goodies.

Then I went to check out the pet supplies aisle.

I saw all kinds of things from chew toys, to dog treats, to dog bones. I started adding anything to my cart that looked appealing. Finally when I got to the end of the aisle, I saw it.

A dog bed.

"Wow," I thought. "This is perfect for Penny."

Without hesitation, I grabbed it and put it in my cart. Then I went to the check-out line to pay for everything. Once I paid for all the stuff, I headed to the parking lot to the car. I got everything loaded and was on my way home.

On the way home, I drove by Elizabeth's old favorite donut shop – "Donuts Galore." I had already passed it when I decided donuts would be good for later on tonight. So when I got to the next street, I turned the corner and came back around. Then I pulled in a parking space, got out, and went in.

When I did, I smelled the familiar scent of fresh brewed coffee. This is where Elizabeth and I would often come to and just relax. She'd always get a cup of coffee with a couple of sour dough donuts. And I'd always get a latte with a few blueberry donuts. We came there so often, there was one employee that worked there that knew us by name.

He was there when I walked in.

"Hey Jake," he called out.

"Hey Anthony."

It took everything I had to get ready for this next question.

"Where's Elizabeth?"

I grit my teeth and looked away while fighting back the tears.

"She passed away."

"What?! Oh no. I'm so sorry to hear that. When did she die?"

"Recently," I responded desparately wanting to just get my donuts and go home.

"Oh my God," he began again. "You two are my favorite customers. I'm sorry, were my favorite customers."

"Yeah, if you don't mind, I'd really rather not talk about it."

"Oh no problem. I'm sorry," he said apologizing again.

"It's O.K. I'll just take two blueberry and two sour dough donuts."

He put the donuts in a bag, purposely trying not to make eye contact.

"That'll be $3.45," he solemnly said.

I paid for it and I didn't try to make eye contact with him either. Then I took the donuts and left.

When I got home and unloaded the car, I put all the groceries up. Then I put Penny's new bed on the floor. She walked up to it, sniffed it, and immediately knew what it was for. She hopped in and curled up.

Then I went to the kitchen to contemplate dinner.

I didn't know why, but I had a taste for macaroni and cheese. So I went to the cabinet and took out a box.

After I cooked it, I prepared my plate and got a can of Sprite out of the refrigerator. Then I sat down and closed my eyes and bowed my head.

"Oh loving and gracious Lord. I thank You for this meal. I thank You for bringing Elizabeth into my life. Even though we didn't get to spend as much time together as we would've liked, I thank You for the time we did have. Also I thank You for Caleb and Shelly. May You bless and enrich their lives and let them spend a lifetime of happiness together. And also I thank You for Penny. For these things I thank You and pray for. Amen."

Then I opened my eyes and began to indulge in my food. When I was done, I put my dishes in the sink and went and turned the lights off and went to my room. I got undressed and put my robe on. Then I went to the living room to say goodnight to Penny. When I got there, she was already sleep. I just stared at her for a moment. Then I whispered, "Goodnight," and went to bed.

ELEVEN

"Stop that. Stop that," I said while laughing half-asleep and half-awake. Then I opened my eyes to see Penny on my pillow licking my face.

I guess this was her way of thanking me for her new bed I bought her yesterday. Then I sat up and picked Penny up and put her on the floor.

I was hungry. But I had to make sure Penny ate first. I went to the kitchen and poured some of her food in her bowl. Then I dished up her water.

Then it hit me. I didn't eat my donuts from yesterday. So I went to the refrigerator and got the bag out. Then I pulled out the carton of milk. I got a cup from the cabinet and sat down at the table. I started with the sour dough ones first. When I was done, I put the milk carton back in the refrigerator and then went to the bedroom. I got my clothes laid out and then headed to the bathroom to have a nice long shower.

I had the water a little hotter than I usually had it. As I stood there and thought, the hot water hit my body soothing me from head to toe.

"Why is all this happening so fast?" I thought.

Then I remembered when I was a kid and whenever something bad would happen, my mom would very blatantly say, "It's something called life. Get over it."

That's exactly what I had to do – get over it.

After my shower, I got dressed and decided to turn in my application. I picked it up off of the dresser, grabbed my keys and headed for the door.

When I got in the car and got my seatbelt fastened, I said out loud. "Elizabeth, I know you're an angel watching me in heaven. I got my fingers crossed that I'll get this job."

Then I started the car up and headed for United Global Finance Company. When I got there, I parked and went in.

The same cool air that was there last time hit me as I entered the front door.

I walked up the receptionist desk and the same lady that was there last time was there again.

I said, "I'd like to turn in my application," handing her the filled out forms.

She then took them and responded, "I'll be sure the hiring manager gets this," while looking at me with unsure eyes.

I then turned and left.

When I stepped outside, it was then and there I realized what a gorgeous day it was. I figured I'd do something fun. Something I hadn't done in a while.

"I got it," I said to myself, but almost thinking out loud. "I'll go to a movie."

Yeah, that's it. I haven't been to a good movie in a long time. Plus when I was watching the previews on T.V. for the new Idris Elba movie, it looked really good.

It was settled; to the movies I was headed. I got in the car and headed for Ward Parkway Theaters.

On the way there, I envisioned me in a comfortable seat with the lights low and a big tub of unhealthy, salty, and buttery popcorn and a large Dr. Pepper.

Oh, this is exactly what I needed!

When I got there and went in, the aroma of the fresh butter popcorn was so tantalizing that it made my mouth water. I went and stood in line to pay for my ticket.

When I finally got up front, I had to describe the movie from what I had seen in the previews and tell that it had Idris Elba in it. The person behind the counter recognized what movie I was referring to and told me the name and rung me up for a ticket. I paid, got my ticket, then went to the ticket-taker.

The ticket-taker took my ticket, tore off the side, and replied, "You'll be in theater four."

"Thank you," I responded. Then I went to get the best part of coming to a movie – popcorn and soda.

I got to the concession stand and asked for a large popcorn and large soda. I paid for it, then went to the condiment stand for salt and butter.

I put plenty of salt and butter on my popcorn. Then I got my Dr. Pepper and was headed for theater four.

When I got there, I found my seat and sat down. Then the lights went low.

Now this is how you have a good time!

As the show went on, I was so entranced that I forgot about all of my troubles as I focused on the movie. I found myself jumping a few times at a few of the scary parts.

Then it was over with an ending that had me on the edge of tears. The lights came on and the credits came up.

As I stood up and stretched, I realized how relieved I had felt. Seeing this show was well worth it and did me a lot of good.

As I was leaving the theater, I saw a man and a woman walking out ahead of me, obviously a couple, and they were remarking on how the movie was so good.

Then I thought to myself, "This is where people come for true enjoyment, but for me it was somewhere I came to forget the pain I was in.

TWELVE

Days passed and no phone call yet for an interview. Soon a few days became an entire week. Still nothing. Finally here I was playing with Penny when the phone rang. I somehow had the feeling this morning when I woke up that I would get a call from them today.

"Hello."

"Hi, may I speak to Mr. Jake Rigsby, please?"

"Speaking, may I ask who's calling?"

"This is Mr. Morris of United Global Finance Company. Recently you turned in an application for employment at our company. I see here you have an Associate's Degree in finance which is a plus. But I was particularly impressed with your experience."

"Oh thank you."

"I'd like you to come in for an interview."

"Sounds great. When should I come?"

"I have an opening on Thursday at 11:00 a.m."

"I'll be there."

"Alright, I'll see you then."

"O.K., and thank you."

"You're very welcome."

"Bye."

"Bye."

I was so excited that when I hung up, I broke out in a victory dance as if I were already hired.

Then I said out loud, "What better way to celebrate than with ice cream?"

I went to the kitchen to dish up a bowl. When I got there, I opened the freezer and pulled out the strawberry ice cream. Then I got a bowl from the cabinet and a spoon from the drawer. I put together the biggest bowl of ice cream I had ever seen. Then I called Penny into the kitchen and dug out a scoop for her and set it on the floor. She quickly began to lick it up. Afterwards I sat down at the table with my ice cream and wasted little time.

Before long I was done and full. Then I looked at my watch and it read 12:30 p.m. It was time for lunch.

But I had just eaten.

That was not a very ideal lunch.

But at least it was something.

Then a fact came across my mind – I needed to go shopping. I decided not to waste any time, so I went to the bedroom and grabbed my wallet and keys and then was out the door.

When I got to the car, before I got in, I suddenly smelled a fragrance. It wasn't just any fragrance though. It was of the same perfume Elizabeth used to wear. I closed my eyes to such fond remembrances of the bitter-sweet memories.

Then I got in the car. At no time at all, I was at the store.

When I got there, I decided to load up on things for the house before even going down the pet aisle. I was able to buy all kinds of things from frozen foods to things you keep in the cabinet. Then I headed to the pet aisle.

As I searched for things for Penny, I only saw things that I had already bought her. So I decided to pay for what I already had in the cart and leave.

When I got to the check-out line and the cashier rung everything up, the total came to a little over one hundred dollars.

"Not bad," I thought. Then I headed to the car and loaded everything up and went home.

When I got home and got everything put up, I slumped on the couch – exhausted.

Then I drifted off.

I drifted off to a place I had never been before.

Where was I?

Wherever it was, it was peaceful. I was on a pallet listening to children laughing and playing. The sky was blue with a gentle summer breeze every now and then wisking by. I could hear the ocean waves meet the shore from time to time, as the birds flew high in the sunlight. As I laid there reading the book entitled, "With Cream Cheese Please," by James Mitchum Oates, I looked to my left and there was Elizabeth right there next to me. I then took her hand and said, "This is how it was supposed to be."

Suddenly I felt something smooth on my finger over and over again. I awakened to see Penny licking my finger.

"Oh, you must be hungry," I said picking her up and taking her to the kitchen.

I then put some Puppy Chow in her bowl and some water. When she was done, I took her for a walk.

While we were out there, I thought about the dream I just had.

How peaceful it was.

Then I wished I could've stayed there forever.

When I was done walking Penny, I went back in to decide on dinner.

When I got in the house, I went straight to the kitchen. As I stood there looking in the cabinets trying to make up my mind as to what I was having, it hit me – I was in the mood for a cold-cut sandwich.

Why not Subway?

With my mind made up, I grabbed my wallet and keys and headed out the door.

When I got there, I knew exactly what I wanted and how I wanted it made.

When I approached the front, there was a man already ahead of me. Then he began, "I'll have the foot-long wheat bread with the cold-cut trio."

The young man behind the counter then responded, "I'm sorry, we don't have the wheat bread and also we're out of the meat for the cold-cut trio."

"Dammit, that's exactly what I wanted," the man said.

Then I started to laugh a little and the man looked at me and he started laughing some too.

"Can you believe it," he jokingly replied to me.

"That's what I wanted too," I responded.

Then he turned his attention back to the young man and began to change his order. When he was done, I ordered mine and left.

When I finally got home, I came in and ate my sandwich and then got ready for bed. When I went back to check on Penny, she was already in her bed sleeping.

Then I went to bed. As I lay there, I thought the first step to moving on and being happy was to not think of Elizabeth so much. So I told myself, "No more dreaming of her. Instead focus on if I get this job. It was right then and there I decided to change how I think. Instead of saying "if" I get this job to "when" I get this job.

Positive thinking.

In no time at all, I was fast asleep.

THIRTEEN

Finally the big day had come – interview day. As I stood in the mirror checking myself from head to toe, I made sure that I was absolutely perfect. That morning, I had a nice long shower and ate a good breakfast.

I knew I was ready.

On the day I got the call from Mr. Morris telling me to come in for the interview was the same day I pulled out the list of possible interview questions and I practiced on good responses to them. Not only that, but I had also been practicing stress-reducing techniques like breathing exercises.

I found that the more I breathed slowly and focused on relaxing, the less stressed and easy going I was.

Then Penny came into the room. I could see her in the mirror just looking at me.

Finally I remarked to her, "Well how do I look?"

She then began licking my pants leg and I took it that she was telling me I looked handsome.

Then came the good part – putting on the cologne.

I took the Stetson off of the drawer and opened it and poured a little in my hand, but careful not to pour too much. Then I splashed it on my clean shaven face and rubbed it in good.

There I stood ready to go.

"Penny, say a prayer for me," I said to her. Then I grabbed my keys, wallet, and my resume and was out the door.

When I got to the big building, I parked and went in. Upon entering, I noticed that the same cool air was present. As I approached the receptionist desk to let them know of my arrival for my interview, I noticed that there was different receptionist than last time. This was definitely a plus because somehow I felt that if it were the same one, it would make me feel very uneasy. Just the way she looked at me when I was there last time made me feel nervous.

"Hi, my name is Jake Rigsby. I'm here for my 11:00 a.m. appointment with Mr. Morris."

"Oh yes," she responded. "If you'll just have a seat, he'll be with you shortly."

"Thank you," I replied then went to take a seat.

As I sat there, I looked at my watch. It read 10:34 a.m.

Definite rule of thumb – always be early to an interview.

But then something happened. I started getting nervous and started thinking the negative "what if's."

What if I stutter while answering his questions? What if I forget the answers to what I practiced? What if I start to sweat? What if he can sense the nervousness and anxiety?

All of this was coming at me now and couldn't have chosen a worse time.

But then I remembered the breathing techniques to reduce stress that I had practiced. So I began. I took a deep breath and let it out slow. Then another and another. As I did this, I focused on relaxing.

It worked!

In no time at all, I was calm and ready to meet Mr. Morris.

A few minutes later, a door opened up and a man in what appeared to be a very expensive suit stepped out. He then looked at me and replied, "Jake Rigsby?"

"Yes, I'm Jake," I responded while standing up.

"I'm John Morris," he said walking up to me with his hand extended.

I then shook his hand.

"Right this way," he said leading me to his office.

When I was close upon him, I could see the wrinkles in his face even though he didn't appear to be that old.

Were the wrinkles from stress I began to wonder?

Is that what working in this job will do to you is stress you out and make you look old before your time?

I began to get cold feet and that nervous feeling started to come back again.

As soon as I got in the office, I noticed that it was cooler in there than in the waiting area. It wasn't an uncomfortable coolness, but it was very soothing.

It made me relax. And then I began to find my focus again.

"Please have a seat," he said as he directed me to a chair in front of his desk. Just the neatness and tidiness and the cool air in his office made everything seem inviting and serene.

He took his seat and began.

He asked me a series of questions. I answered them as calmly and plainly as I had rehearsed. When he got to the part about my experience, I felt it best not to lie, but to stretch the truth a bit.

"And here," he finally said, "I see you have an Associate's Degree in Finance. That is certainly good."

Then he explained to me just what it was that they did in the company and if I were hired, what I would be doing. Everything he said sounded so positive, it made me think that I already had the job.

Then he said, "I'm not going to beat around the bush. You're exactly what we're looking for at this company. And also any man who likes Stetson, in my opinion, has excellent taste. You're hired."

I couldn't believe my ears.

"I'm hired?" I ecstatically said.

"Yes, can you be here Monday at 9:00 a.m.?"

"Definitely."

"Alright," he said standing up and extending his hand. I stood up and shook his hand.

"Thank you and you won't be disappointed," I said.

Then I turned to leave.

FOURTEEN

All I did until Monday came was ate healthy and pray. Then the big day came. Penny lay curled up on my pillow while I stood in the mirror.

"Remember, don't talk too much but just enough so they won't think you're an outcast," I said out loud while straightening my tie.

"And if they try to get too personal, just politely let them know it's none of their business."

Naw, too subtle.

Just relax. Take a deep breath.

"Well, how do I look?" I said to Penny while still looking in the mirror.

When she raised her head up and looked at me, I took that as a positive response. Then I grabbed my keys and wallet and was out the door.

When I got there and got in the parking lot and finally parked and turned the car off, I took my hands off the steering wheel to see some wetness where I was holding the wheel.

My hands had been sweating. I was more nervous than I thought.

Take a deep breath.

Then I went into the huge building.

When I got in, the first thing I did was look at my watch. It said 8:47 a.m. Then I saw Mr. Morris standing at his office door. I walked to him and when I got there I saw another man standing in his office.

"Jake, this is Bob Mathers," Mr. Morris began.

"Pleased to meet you," I said extending my hand to shake his.

"Likewise," he replied extending his hand as well.

Something about this guy was kind-of weird.

"Bob will be training you on your first day," Mr. Morris announced.

Then I figured out what it was that was so weird about this guy.

I recognized him.

He was the same guy that was at Subway that one night who wanted the cold-cut trio on wheat bread.

"Do I know you from somewhere?" Bob said sensing that I looked familiar.

"Yes, I was the guy at Subway the night you were there and they were out of wheat bread and the cold-cut trio."

"Oh yes," he responded.

I could hear the inflection in his voice raise a little.

"Small world, isn't it?" I replied.

"Yes, it sure is," he happily agreed.

"Well the two of you should get along fine," Mr. Morris finally interjected. "Jake, I'm leaving you in the hands of Bob."

Then Mr. Morris left.

Looks like I was off to a pretty decent start.

"So you like Subway?" Bob nonchalantly asked.

I thought it was unprofessional to indulge in small talk on the first day at work. But so as to make a good impression and to not offend him, I decided to humor him.

"Yeah, Subway is O.K. It's not my first choice of favorite foods though. I'm more of a burger man myself."

"You know that's the same with me."

I could sense that he was lying just to get on my good side.

"So what'll we be doing today?" I asked changing the conversation.

"Well there are just a few things I want to go over with you. The job is not hard at all," he said stepping out of the office. "Right this way."

"I'll show you where you'll be working," he said walking ahead of me.

Finally we reached an office.

"Here we are," he announced.

When I walked in, I noticed it was spatious but cozy. But more importantly, it had cool air.

"You can decorate it anyway you like," Bob said as I explored my new space.

"This is wonderful," I exclaimed.

"Now we'll be going over what you'll be doing," Bob responded.

As he talked, I was somewhat there, but somewhat wasn't. I kept focusing on and imagining how to decorate my new office. Also I kept envisioning me actually being and working in my newly decorated office. I was able to comprehend most of what Bob said, but the rest I figured I'd pick up on my own. So when Bob was finally done and he asked, "So do you have any questions of me?" I responded, "No."

He then said, "O.K., we'll just be practicing today and we'll continue practicing for about a week and I'll monitor you and then from there you should be good to go."

"Thanks Bob."

"Don't mention it."

FIFTEEN

That night, I lay in bed – tired. I didn't bother to eat dinner. I was so anxious and excited about this new job, that I didn't notice my hunger.

Then my phone rang.

"Hello."

"Hey Jake."

"Oh hey, Caleb."

"Do you have time to talk?"

"Honestly, not really. I just started this new job and I have to be there in the morning. And also I'm exhausted from playing with Penny for a while."

"Oh."

"But hey, we can talk," I said sensing his disappointment.

"Yeah, I just called to check on you and see how you're doing."

"I'm doing great. I just started this new job. And Penny is doing great too."

"That's good. I just want to make sure you're O.K. and supporting yourself."

"Yep, couldn't be better."

"Alright, well Shelly and the kids send their love."

"That's good. Give them a big hug and kiss for me."

"You got it, bro."

"O.K., love ya."

"Love you too, little bro."

"Bye."

"Bye."

When I got off the phone with Caleb, I put the phone on the dresser and in no time at all, I was sleep.

I awakened to the music of my alarm clock going off. As soon as I did, I sat up and hit the button. It said 6:00 a.m. As I was sitting up in my bed, an unusually weird feeling came over me. It actually wasn't unusually weird as it was good.

Then it hit me.

I felt refreshed and revived.

I had never in my life felt as refreshed as this. It was right then and there I knew today would be a really good day. I hopped out of bed and went to go feed Penny. After Penny ate, I took her for her walk, then came in and headed for the kitchen.

I didn't eat dinner last night and I heard my stomach grumbling. I really had a taste for eggs, so I scrambled some up and made two pieces of toast and a cup of coffee.

Before eating, I said a nice long prayer thanking the Lord for the meal I had in front of me. Then I indulged.

When I was done, I set my dishes in the sink and then headed to the bathroom to take my shower.

When I was done with that, I got dressed. As I stood in the mirror admiring myself, I remembered, "Can't forget the

Stetson." I poured some in my hand and then rubbed it onto my face.

I then looked at the clock. I had plenty of time to spare before I had to go in. I decided to get the pictures that I would put in my office.

I went to the closet. I pulled out a box and opened it up. In there were documents, but no pictures. I closed it and set it back in the closet. Then I pulled the next box out and opened it up. Here were tons of pictures. I began flipping through them.

I came across one of me and Elizabeth. We each had an ice cream cone in our hand. I remember when we took it, we had a nice man, whom we did not know, to take the photo for us.

"I definitely need to get a frame for this one," I said to myself.

I continued to look and search for other pictures of me and Elizabeth together. Then I came across one with me, Elizabeth, and Penny.

We looked so happy.

Then the tears began to well up. It was then that I remembered that I was going to try and have an excellent day and the way I felt this morning. So I wiped my eyes of the tears and set the box aside.

"You got this," I whispered.

Then I headed to work.

SIXTEEN

An entire week had finally passed and I had been working this job under Bob's training. I had finally bought the frames for the pictures I had chosen to decorate my office with. I was so excited about how my office would look, that in some remote sense, I thought about it as my home away from home.

"Good morning, Bob," I very cheerily replied as I walked in and saw him standing at the receptionist desk.

"Oh good morning, Jake," he responded just as enthusiastically as I had to him.

As I approached him, he turned his attention to the receptionist and said, "Now I'll need those no later than Wednesday so I need you to get right on it as soon as possible."

"Sure thing," she replied.

Then I stood in front of Bob. I could sense that he wanted to shake my hand, but he didn't even extend his hand because he saw that in one of my hands was a briefcase that I had brought to carry all of my important papers in. In the other hand was a bag in which I had my pictures and decorations to spruce up my office with.

Without anything else to say, I walked to my office.

When I got there, I set everything down and closed the door. Then I pulled out my decorations and began.

The first thing I pulled out was a fake plant. I set it on the corner of my desk for the time being. Then I looked at it for a moment and finally decided, "That's the perfect place for it – on the corner of my desk."

The next thing I pulled out was a picture of me and Elizabeth. I then happened to look at the wall and noticed that there were some nails that had been embedded in them.

This was obviously because the person that worked in this office before me had pictures that they had hung on the walls.

I found a nice spot on the wall and hung the pictures there.

Then I pulled out a picture of Caleb, Shelly, and their children. I put my hand on my chin and said, "Hmmm," contemplating on where would be the best place to put it.

Then I thought, "Why not here in the other corner across from the plant." When I set it there, I stepped back to look at it.

Perfect!

Then I went and pulled out another picture. This one was of mom. I looked up at the wall at the picture of me and Elizabeth and decided this one should probably go across from it. Also there was a nail in the wall where I wanted to hang it. I put it up there and looked at it.

I miss you mom.

Then I went and pulled out a picture of me, Elizabeth, and Penny. I decided to set that one right at the very front of the desk.

Then I pulled out the last picture. It was of Penny by herself. I decided to set that one in front too across from the last one.

There I had it; my new office.

Then I looked at my watch and saw how much time I spent decorating and realized I had to get some work done. I sat down and logged into my computer and began.

I was working and working for what seemed like a while until my stomach began to grumble. I looked at my watch and it read 11:55 a.m.

"Not a minute too soon," I thought.

Then a knock on the door.

"Come in," I replied.

The door opened and in stepped Bob.

"Hey Bob."

"Hey Jake. I was just coming to check on you. How's everything going?"

"Oh, it's going fine."

"Wow, this is nice," Bob exclaimed while looking around at my newly decorated office. He looked at each picture and had a good comment for each one. He even had something good to say about the fake plant.

Then he saw the pictures of Penny with me and Elizabeth and the picture of Penny by herself both sitting in front.

"This is your dog, I take it?" he said looking at the picture of Penny by herself.

"Yeah, that's Penny."

"I thought the wife or mom was supposed to be up front," he said obviously joking.

"Yeah, I just want to see my Penny as much as possible. It's not enough when I don't see her by working here when I do."

"Hmmm interesting."

There was silence for a few seconds.

"Well at any rate, I was wondering if maybe you'd like to grab a bite to eat."

"Sure, where to?"

"How 'bout Subway?"

SEVENTEEN

Both Bob and I timed out for our break and then we were on our way to Subway.

We decided to take Bob's car.

When we got to his car and he unlocked it and I got in, the first thing I noticed was a musty odor. He got in and I tried to avoid crinkling my nose as if signifying my displeasure to the scent. So instead, I said, "You know what? It's such a gorgeous day today, why don't we roll down the windows?"

"Ah, that's what this is for," Bob replied flipping on the AC.

"Perfect," I thought. Now the smell began to spread and get stronger.

I almost lost my appetite!

Then we were headed for Subway.

When we got there and he parked, I almost hopped out of the car for fear of if I was in there another second, I would've vomited.

Bob, sensing that something was wrong, asked, "Is everything O.K.?"

"Sure," I said trying to make sure my lie went undetected. "I was just a little hungry."

Then we went in.

When we got in, the aroma of fresh baked bread hit my nostrils and replaced the undesirable scent of Bob's car. We stepped up to the counter to order.

"Hi, welcome to Subway," the girl behind the counter said.

"Hi," Bob responded. I'll have the Italian BMT on wheat bread with the foot long."

"And you, sir?" the girl said addressing her attention to me.

"I'll have the meatball marinara on wheat bread with the foot long."

After we got our sandwiches fixed, we both decided on a bag of chips for each of us. Then we got drinks and found a table.

When we sat down, we both began to eat. Neither one of us said grace.

"So," Bob began, "that picture I saw in your office of you and that woman; was that Mrs. Jake?"

"She was, but not anymore," I somberly said.

"Divorced?"

"Deceased."

"Oh, I'm sorry to hear that," Bob said pausing on his chewing for a moment. I could hear the remorse in his voice.

"How'd she die?" Bob asked with a frown on his face obviously concerned.

"Lung cancer."

"Oh, I'm sorry to hear that."

"How 'bout you? Are you married?"

"Yeah, to my precious, Jill. Next week is our seven year anniversary. We always go out of the way for each other for the anniversary."

Then I thought back to how Elizabeth and I set our marriage date to be on the same day we met so that we'd always feel that same magic we shared when we both first saw each other.

I was thinking and thinking when Bob finally piped up, "This sandwich is really good. How's yours?"

He could tell I was lost.

"Oh, it's really good; just the way a sandwich should taste."

"Any kids?" Bob curiously asked.

"No, how 'bout you?"

"Yeah, I have a four-year-old boy. He's a mama's boy. In fact I think the only thing he took after me is the fact that he is a mama's boy. When I was his age, I was the same way. I really did love my mom."

"Yeah, same here. I was always looking for the affection of my mom over my dad."

"Interesting," Bob said as if analyzing me.

"Now I have no one in my life. I don't have my mom or my wife. All I have is Penny."

"Penny is the dog in the picture in your office?"

"Yep, if I didn't have her, I wouldn't know what to do."

"Interesting," Bob said once again still analyzing me.

Then I began rambling on about Penny and the things that I buy for her. When I was done talking, I saw the quizzical look on Bob's face. In his eyes I saw questions – questions that he wanted answered.

EIGHTEEN

Months passed and here I was working my new job and enjoying every bit of it. Bob and I became the best of friends. He was always questioning me about Elizabeth and the times we shared. He was assessing me pretty good – or just being nosy.

I was on my computer when I looked at my watch and it said 12:07 p.m.

Then a knock at the door.

"Come in," I said.

Bob opened the door and stuck his head in and replied, "Hey, I'm headed for lunch. Did you wanna come?"

"Sure, gimme a second. I'm just shutting my computer down."

"I was thinking how 'bout Wendy's today?"

"Sounds good," I said standing up as my computer was shutting down.

Then we headed to Wendy's.

When we got there and went in, I knew exactly what I wanted. Apparently Bob did too.

He approached the counter and began, "I'll have the Big Bacon Classic Combo."

The young man behind the counter rung it up and Bob paid for it and got his cup.

Then I began, "I'll have the Spicy Chicken Sandwich Combo."

After I was rung up, I paid for mine and got my cup.

While we were getting our drinks, the young man then replied, "Your order is ready."

I turned to see our food sitting on trays on the counter.

"Boy, that was fast," Bob replied.

"That's why it's called fast food," I responded.

Then we got our trays and found a table.

When we sat down, Bob unwrapped his sandwich.

"So tell me the latest news. Anything exciting and new going on?" Bob asked.

"No, not really."

Then he began asking questions about Elizabeth and past memories.

"Alright enough with the past. I'd really rather not focus on Elizabeth. She's dead and the more I talk about her, the more emotional I get."

He could sense a little irritation in my voice.

"Well you spend so much time talking about Penny, I was just wondering if you can think about dating or finding a new love and not just focusing on your dog."

"Are you suggesting I'm sleeping with Penny?"

"No, no, I'm just saying that maybe it's time to stop feeling down and get back in the swing of things. You're a very handsome guy. I know a lot of women on the job who would love to date you. People talk, you know?"

"Really?"

"Oh yeah. It's time to get going again. You've buried your wife, now bury the pain."

"That's really motivating."

"Now eat up, your sandwich is getting cold."

NINETEEN

The years came and went and as they did, I enjoyed working each and every day. Then more time had passed and before I knew it, I had been working there an entire eight years.

Bob was very so often and very steadily trying to get me set up with one of the females on the job. He was always telling me that several of them had the "hots" for me.

Although I never saw proof that this was true nor had I reason to believe it.

Until one day I was at the fax machine down the hall from my office. I had just got done faxing some forms and I had a warm cup of coffee in my hand. As I turned around, there was Joyce standing very close behind me; so close, I bumped into her and spilled my coffee. It got all over my pants.

"Oh, I'm sorry. What an idiotic thing to do," I apologetically said.

"Oh, it's O.K.," she replied accepting my apology as if it were my fault.

Then she started wiping my pants with her bare hands – very close to my thigh.

Then in the back of my mind, I thought, "I haven't been this close to a woman in a long time."

Then I began to get all jittery and fumbly. As I bent down to pick up my cup, she bent down too, to pick up her ink pen she dropped. But as we were both raising up to stand up, about midway of standing up, my face was right there at her breasts. I could see the busty and curviness of her round huge breasts.

I was ecstatic!

It was obvious she wanted me. All I had to do was just talk to her.

But then that shy little boy in me took over and I said, "Have a nice day, Joyce." Then I hurriedly walked to my office. When I got there, I closed my door behind me and slumped in my chair.

What just happened?

I sat there for about ten minutes just trying to cool down.

Then a knock at my door.

"Who is it?" I asked.

"It's Bob," the voice from behind the door said.

"Oh come in."

Bob came in and saw me sitting there slumped in my chair.

"Are you O.K.? You look different."

"Of course I'm not O.K. Let me tell you what just happened. I was at the fax machine faxing my report and when I turned around, there was Joyce close to me – dangerously close. I bumped into her and spilled my coffee on my pants. Then she began wiping my pants with her bare hand and she was extremely close to my thigh. Then when I bent down to pick my cup up off the floor and she bent down as well to pick up her ink pen, it was like she was showing me her breasts.

"And what'd you do?"

"What could I do? I got all nervous and wired up and told her to have a nice day and then I walked away."

"Yeah, that's what any smooth operator would've done."

"This is no time for jokes. I mean Joyce really wanted me."

"Well what are you doing sitting here? Go talk to her."

"In case you haven't noticed, it's been eight years I've been here and I haven't approached one female here. I just have a hard time expressing romantic sentiment."

"Well you're not into that other thing, are you?"

"What other thing?"

"Well you said you have a hard time with the ladies. You're not into guys, are you?"

"What? No listen, I'm not gay. It's just that I've always been a little shy."

"Oh."

"And not only that, but I feel kind-of wrong about fraternizing with co-workers. It just doesn't feel right."

"Doesn't feel right? It couldn't be more right. Let me tell you, some of the things I've done in the past that count for wrongness makes you look like a saint. It's just a little fooling around on the job. It's not like anyone's going to get fired. I'll tell you what, just think about it."

"Well Bob, I pretty much got my mind made up on this one. I just want to keep it one hundred percent professional."

"Suit yourself."

TWENTY

"Well Penny, another day, another dollar," I said straightening out my tie. I was just about to head for the door, when I realized I was forgetting something – the Stetson.

This is what probably got me hired in the first place.

I splashed some on and was out the door.

When I got to work, there was Bob at my office door waiting on me.

"Hey Bob," I said as I was approaching him.

"Hey Jake. Just the man I want to see," he heartily replied.

I thought to myself, "He's in an awfully good mood today."

I just wanted to apologize if I seemed a little pushy with the incident with Joyce."

"Pushy?"

"Yeah well, it's just that I know that you have your standards and if I seemed a little over-bearing when I was trying to get you to score with Joyce, I'm sorry. Plus you were right about not getting sexually involved with co-workers."

"Oh, it's O.K."

"So how have you been aside from that?"

"You know, I must say, I've been doing really good. I've been eating healthier and also I've started meditating."

"Really? How's that working out for you?"

"O.K., I guess. The only thing is I don't know if I'm doing it right. But it really calms me."

"If you don't know if you're doing it right, why not just study it or research the proper methods? I'm sure there are tons of things on google."

"Well, I really don't think it's necessary. I mean how hard can it be? Just close your eyes and relax. Right?"

"It's a little more to it than that. Not only that, but once you start doing it exactly the right way, I'm sure you'll feel a hell of a lot less stressed."

"Maybe," I said glancing at my watch. "You know, I'm really behind on my paperwork," I replied politely trying to let Bob know that I wanted to get to my work.

"Oh sure," Bob said as I entered the office. He then stuck his head in the doorway and asked, "We still on for lunch?"

"Sure thing."

At 12:00 p.m. exactly, a knock at the door.

"Come in," I replied.

The door opened and Bob stepped in.

"You just about ready?" he asked.

"Yeah, just gimme a second. There we go," I said finally getting my computer to shut down. "Where are we headed today," I asked. "I'm so hungry I could eat anything."

"How does pizza sound?"

"Sounds great."

"This isn't just any pizza though. This is Dewey's Pizzeria, where real pizza is made."

"My mouth is already watering."

Bob and I went to Dewey's Pizzeria. I ate so much, I thought my stomach would bust. When we got back to work, I went to my office and sat down. Never had I been so full.

I longed to go home so I could stretch out in my bed and relax.

Finally when it was time to go home, I didn't waste any time logging off of my computer.

Then I headed home.

When I got home and got to my door and pulled my key out, something was deathly wrong.

The door was cracked open a little bit. I grabbed the knob and it was loose and wobbly as if it had been pounded on.

Someone broke in my home!

I didn't know if the intruders were still there, nor did I care.

My only concern at that time was Penny.

I rushed in.

"Penny," I called out. "Penny where are you?"

I got to my bedroom. When I did, I heard a sound from the closet.

I thought, "Oh my God! Someone might be hiding there waiting on me."

Without thought, I opened the closet door prepared to face death.

When I did, out came Penny. She jumped up on me and started licking me. I began caressing and rubbing her. I became so engrossed in the fact that Penny was alright, I forgot that the intruder might still be in the house. Realizing this, I searched the entire house from top to bottom. As I searched, I took little mental notes of the damage done and what was taken.

Then I called the police.

TWENTY-ONE

It took them a while to get there, but hearing the sirens pulling up outside gave me a great peace of mind.

Seconds later, they were at the door.

The door was still part way open when the first officer walked in and saw me standing there.

"We got a call in about a robbery," the officer said.

"Yes, when I came home, the door was open and a few of my things were missing," I responded.

"Well we'll take a look around," the officer replied. And then two other officers came in.

They searched and looked around the entire house. Then when one of them got to the bedroom, he called out, "Oh man, who's this?"

"That's just my dog, Penny."

"She's not vicious," he replied.

"No, I didn't train her that way," I responded.

"Which is not a good thing because if she were an attack dog, the burglars would've never made it in."

I thought the officer was insinuating that I wasn't a good pet owner.

"Can we just speed this up?" I said with irritation in my voice.

"Yeah sure," one of the other officers said.

Five minutes later they came back to me.

"From what you saw, was there much stolen?" one of them asked.

"No, not much at all. Just a few things," I replied.

While two of the officers asked me questions, the other one was writing down my responses on his pad.

When they were done, the officer who was doing the writing said, "O.K., we'll fill out a report and we'll be in touch. In the meantime, it would help if you trained your dog to watch the house."

"Thank you," I replied.

Then they left.

The next day I went and bought a new lock for the door. Then I sat down to have a talk with Penny. She sat there, ears perked up – listening.

"Penny, I'm going to need you to be the eyes and ears of the house when I'm not here. If someone comes through that door other than me, you attack."

She started wagging her tail.

I took that as a sign that she understood.

I called in sick that morning because I was too embarrassed to tell them the truth; that someone had broken into my home.

After my talk with Penny, all I did was sleep – all day long. Needless to say, I was very well rested for the next day at work.

I was working in my office when Bob came in. He didn't even knock.

"Hey Jake."

"Hey Bob."

"Are you feeling any better? I heard you were sick yesterday."

"Bob, can you close the door for a minute?"

"Yeah sure," he said closing the door.

"Alright Bob, the truth is I wasn't sick at all yesterday. I got robbed."

"Are you O.K.? They didn't hurt you, did they?"

"No, I didn't get robbed, my house did. Someone broke in my home."

"Oh no."

"Yeah, but the amazing thing is, they didn't take much at all."

"Was Penny O.K.?"

"Yeah, she was fine. She was hiding in the closet."

"Thank God for that. You know what? Today's your lucky day. I have something for you. It's in my office. No one has ever seen it. I'll get it for you. But you can't tell anyone I gave you this."

"You have my promise."

Bob left and then came back a few minutes later. He didn't have anything with him.

"Where is it?" I inquired.

"Right here," Bob said digging inside of the front of his pants.

Then he pulled out a gun.

"I've never had to use it so I think you'll find more use for it than me."

"Bob, I don't know what to say."

"You're welcome."

TWENTY-TWO

Boy, was it beautiful. As I sat on my bed polishing my new gun, I couldn't help but think to myself, "How many lives has this thing taken or how many people has it hurt?" I know Bob said he never had to use it, but could he be lying.

It was morning time. All night long, I slept with the gun underneath my pillow. It was safe because I had unloaded it before going to bed. Although that probably wasn't the best idea because if the intruders came back and I was there, I would be totally unprepared with an unloaded gun.

I finally decided to keep it loaded and leave it on my dresser.

Suddenly my mind began to wander. It wandered back to Joyce. Then the oddest thing occurred to me about how Bob was always trying to set me up with and go out with the different females on the job.

So after all the time I had been working there, not once, ever had Joyce shown any sexual likings to or interest in me whatsoever. Then all of a sudden, out of the clear blue, she comes on to me like crazy.

The only other notion I could get from this is Bob put her up to it.

My blood began to boil.

I told myself even before I had started working, that I would keep it one hundred percent professional.

Which explicitly meant no interpersonal relations with the other employees and certainly nothing sexual.

I was tempted to call Bob right then and there and straighten him out. But then I thought, "No, it's better if I confront him and talk to him face to face."

I looked at my clock and realized that I'd better hurry and get dressed or I'd be late for work. I hopped up and went to the bathroom to take my shower. When I was done, I got dressed. I decided that there was no time for breakfast. So I got all of my stuff and headed out the door.

When I got there and walked in, I saw Bob at the end of the hall. I then began to approach him with meaningful strides.

At last I was right behind him.

I tapped him on the shoulder.

He turned around and I began, "Hey Bob," I said with much irritation in my tone, "why'd you do it?"

"Jake, what are you talking about?"

"You know damn well what I'm talking about. You set Joyce up to come on to me."

"Oh that."

"Yeah that."

"Listen, why are you getting all worked up for? You should be thanking me."

"Thanking you?!"

"Yeah, I just figured you could use a little sex for yourself. No big deal."

"That's none of your goddamn business!"

"Hey Jake, I'm sorry. I didn't mean to offend you."

"Oh yeah, well how's this for offend? I quit!"

When I said that, I turned and began to walk away. As I walked, I could feel years and years of pent up frustration and hurt over Elizabeth's death guiding me. This was the frustration and hurt that I never released and let go. So it just stayed inside of me all that time; just bottled up waiting to be released.

But was this the real reason I had just screamed at Bob and then quit my job – because of the pain from Elizabeth's death that I never let go.

Before I knew it, I was outside the building. I got in my car and drove away and didn't look back.

TWENTY-THREE

I don't know what time I went to bed last night, but I know I must've been awfully tired because I didn't wake up until 11:03 a.m.

Here I was lying in bed wondering what did hell did I quit my job for? Not only that, but I had a terrible headache. Something told me to take some Tylenol and go back to bed. But I couldn't just lay around all day. I had things to do. I got up and fed Penny.

After we came back from her walk, I decided to call Caleb. But then I thought, "Naw, he'll just ask how's the job going and the last thing I want to tell him is that I quit. He'll think that I need money and the last thing I want to be is a dependent.

Then the phone rang.

"Hello."

"Hello Jake. This is John Morris."

"Oh, hi John."

I knew he would be calling eventually.

"Yes Jake, I understand that you quit working here. May I ask the reason why?"

"Yeah, I guess I just couldn't deal with Bob trying to set me up with another employee."

"I heard all about that and I do apologize for that. But the truth is Jake, that we need you here at the company.

You're our strongest employee. The quotas you've made are outstanding. I guess I'm just asking you to reconsider your decision upon resignation."

"I'll think about it, John."

"Well when you decide, let me know."

"Alright."

"O.K. bye."

"Bye."

I then got up to go to the kitchen to fix a snack. When I got there, I saw something very odd. Penny was just lying on the floor – in the same spot Elizabeth died. I went to her and called her name and even though she did not respond, I saw her rib cage going up and down letting me know that she was breathing.

I then rubbed her side. She raised her head, but then put it back down.

Something was definitely wrong. I decided to take her to the vet.

Penny was diagnosed with intestinal cancer and just like my Elizabeth not long to live.

I stood there and pleaded, "Isn't there something you can do, something?"

"I'm afraid not. The cancer has set in too far for any treatment to help at all. I'm sorry."

I wouldn't take no for an answer. So I left her at the vet and told them I would pay any fee necessary, just help my Penny.

A week later, I got a call from the vet at 7:36 p.m. telling me that Penny had died. I didn't know what to do. I became beside myself. The same beast that took my wife away from me also took Penny.

I had nothing left.

So I took out the loaded gun that Bob gave me and I put it to my temple.

But then I thought, "This is crazy. I'm certainly not going to kill myself."

I put the gun back on the drawer and climbed in bed and went to sleep.

The next morning when I awakened, I heard a noise in the living room. I thought it might be an intruder so I went to check it out.

And lo and behold, there was Penny. I then fed her and got her leash ready to take her for a walk.

EPILOGUE

The coroner's report said the bullet lodged through Jake's brain killing him instantly on impact. He was laid to rest and family and friends were at the funeral. As for Bob, he was never caught for his misdeeds. What did he do wrong? He hired some thugs to break into Jake's house with the intent to kill Penny with hopes that if Penny were gone, then Jake could learn to live a little more by having fun and dating. But now Jake and Penny are both in heaven. The funeral wasn't hard to plan because Jake already told Caleb, "When I die, I want to be buried next to Penny."

CPSIA information can be obtained
at www.ICGtesting.com
Printed in the USA
BVHW071404100720
583431BV00001B/126